BACKYARD WITCH

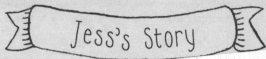

Jess's Story

by Christine Heppermann and Ron Koertge

illustrated by Deborah Marcero

Greenwillow Books, *An Imprint of* HarperCollins *Publishers*

Backyard Witch: Jess's Story
Text copyright © 2016 by Christine Heppermann and Ron Koertge;
illustrations copyright © 2016 by Deborah Marcero
For information address HarperCollins Children's Books, a division of HarperCollins Publishers, 195 Broadway, New York, NY 10007.
www.harpercollinschildrens.com
The text of this book is set in Berling Roman.
Book design by Sylvie Le Floc'h

Library of Congress Control Number: 2017903386
Heppermann, Christine, author.
Jess's story / by Christine Heppermann and Ron Koertge ; pictures by Deborah Marcero.
pages cm.—(Backyard witch ; #2)
"Greenwillow Books."

ISBN 978-0-06-233841-9 (trade ed.)— ISBN 978-0-06-233842-6 (pbk. ed.)

17 18 19 20 21 CG/OPM 10 9 8 7 6 5 4 3 2 1
First paperback edition, 2017

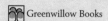 Greenwillow Books

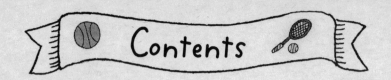

Contents

Chapter 1
Food, Blah, Blah, Food

Jess drummed on the underside of the table.

Taptaptap. Tap-tap-tap. Taptaptap.

SOS—the Morse code distress signal. Not that there was a chance her best friends, Sadie and Maya, would burst through the double doors of the banquet hall, past the row of waiters in their short red jackets, to

rescue her. But her only other option was to die of boredom or starvation or both, soooooo . . .

Taptaptap. Tap-tap-tap. Taptaptap.

The very tall woman seated to her right sniffed. To her left, her mother stopped chatting with a red-faced man and gave Jess a look. A look that said, *You remember what we talked about, don't you?*

Jess nodded and picked up the menu.

Beneath *A Celebration of Chefs*, printed in swooping gold cursive, came the list: first, crab cakes. Then eels. Baby eels. In garlic sauce.

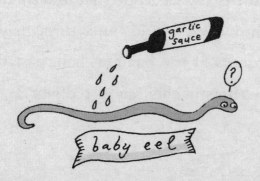

garlic sauce

?

baby eel

She may have made the teensiest, tiniest gagging sound.

This time her mother's look had a lot more capital letters: *You Remember What We Talked About, Don't You?*

"Mom, are they going to announce the awards soon?" *So we can get out of here and go home.*

"Be patient."

"I *am* being patient. I'm just asking."

"Your daughter is *très charmant*," said the red-faced man.

"She's *très* something," replied her mother. Then in a brighter tone, "Jess, I was telling Chef Rénard that I used to test my recipes on you when you were a baby." Her mother turned toward the red-faced man and smiled. "She ate everything I put in front of her. Quinoa with Parmesan and dill. Lemon prune whip."

"Such a sophisticated palate for a little one," murmured Chef Rénard.

"You whipped a prune." Jess grimaced. "And made me eat it?"

"You banged on your high chair tray when I didn't spoon it in fast enough." Her mother and Chef Rénard laughed together. Jess ignored them and studied the centerpiece.

She identified a pineapple and . . . was that an artichoke? She was so  hungry, she could almost eat them. Well, maybe just the pineapple.

Good thing she'd brought—as Maya would say—provisions.

"So," her mother continued. "I named my catering business after my first and most important client. J. B. Catering. The 'J. B.' stands for Jessica Blair."

Before her mother could launch into another thrilling story from her past—first diaper rash? first tooth?—Jess asked, "May I go to the bathroom?"

She wound her way through the maze of banquet tables, each one full of chattering chefs. Some were young. Some weren't. Some had tattoos twining out from under their shirt sleeves or climbing up from their collars. She caught bits of conversation— food, food, *blah*, *blah*, *blah*, *blah*, food.

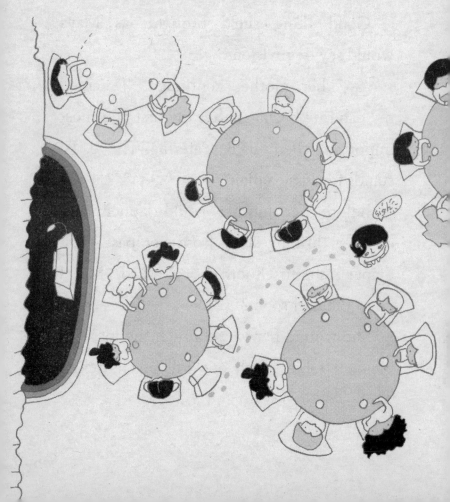

At one table a boy her age or a little older sat looking down and smiling, and not because he was enchanted by his swan-shaped napkin. She'd give anything to be playing Cookie Smoosh or Pirate Party right now, but no way would her

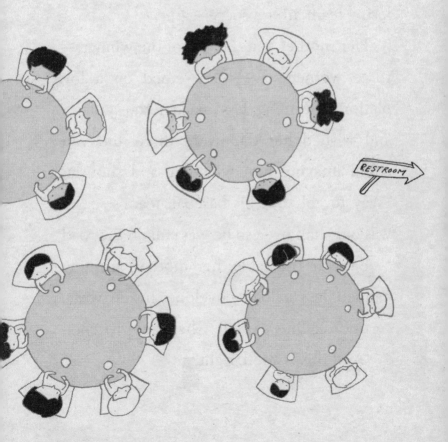

mother hand over her precious phone.

Jess returned just as the names were being called. Her mother's was first! The other chefs at the table shook her mother's hand, but limply, like they didn't mean it. Like the losing team after a soccer game.

Her mother and the rest of the winners—three women, two men—stood on a low platform, beaming. Jess joined in the applause and wished her dad were there, too. She could imagine him whistling and shouting "Way to go!" But his baseball team's season was only half over, so he was still on the road.

Back at the table, her mother, grinning, handed Jess a long envelope. Inside was a certificate: One Week in Chef Paul's Kitchen.

"And this is good, right?"

"Chef Paul is famous, honey. It's a privilege to have an opportunity to work beside him. I'll learn a lot."

"By cutting up his vegetables?"

"Let's talk about this later."

Jess poked the edge of the tablecloth, which was as white as milk. Maybe whiter. She lifted the heavy silver fork. A waiter tried to set a plate of crab cakes in front of her. Cakes. Made out of crab. That was just so . . . wrong. "Could I maybe have a salad instead?" she asked.

"Of course," said the waiter.

Her mother tilted her head in concentration as she tasted the crab cakes and then said to her neighbor, "Maybe a tad too much mustard."

He made a humming sound as he rolled his eyes toward the ceiling. "Hmmm. Or not enough. The balance is certainly off."

The waiter set down Jess's salad. She took a bite of lettuce. Looked thoughtful. Looked at the ceiling. "Hmmm. Either too much of something or not enough of something else."

Her mother used the Warning Voice. "Jess."

Jess picked at her salad, moving little strange things to one side of her plate where they could all be strange together. In a room full of copycats, all sitting very straight, tasting deliberately, rolling their eyes in unison, she thought of her friends. If only she were with them right now. Maya spelling words twice as long as grown-up eels. Sadie identifying every bird in the neighborhood.

Away went the salad and the crab cake plates. Waiters moved fast. Jess moved fast, too, especially on soccer fields and tennis courts. A natural athlete, her father said. And he should know. But she'd never want to be a waiter. That would mean, well, waiting. And it was indoors.

As the waiter served the lamb, Jess shook her head politely. He bent toward her and whispered, "What if I bring you something vegetarian?"

"I'm not really a vegetarian, but that would be great. Thanks."

The very tall woman said, "You don't like lamb, dear?"

"I just remembered that its fleece was white as snow," she replied. "Once."

The woman smiled in that annoying way grown-ups do. Jess vowed never to smile like that. Ever. She knew the word for that smile, thanks to Maya. It was *condescending*. To look down on. There was "descend" right in the middle.

"Jess, how are you getting along?"

"I'm fine, Mom. The waiter is bringing me something that didn't run around with its friends and go '*Baaa*.'"

Her mother's eyes narrowed just as the waiter leaned in and presented Jess with a bowl of soup. Or she hoped it was soup. It looked like a small pond covered with scum.

"Promise me there isn't something hiding in there," she said to the waiter. "Something long and squirmy whose name begins with 'E.'"

"No worries. It's watercress puree."

"Um, yum?"

The waiter laughed and hurried away. Jess tried the soup. It didn't taste bad exactly, just . . . green. Alien life-form green. Pus-draining-from-the-monster's-eyes green.

She put down her spoon.

The very tall woman picked up a different spoon and asked, "May I?" More eye rolling. Then, "Very nice, actually. It looks simple, but if the cress is blanched too much or not enough, you have to start all over."

"Don't I know it," said Jess. "I can't tell you how many times I've blanched my cress too much."

Now her mother's look had exclamation points!

When the eels arrived, Jess pushed her plate to the side. She was hungry, though. She felt all buzzy and hollow, like a balloon filled with bees. Her backpack was tucked away right at her feet. So she reached for it.

The zipper opened quietly, and what she wanted, what she'd hidden there, sat right on top. Silently she lifted the sandwich in its waxed paper up to the table. Surreptitiously—one of Maya's favorite words—she slid it onto a small white plate and began to unwrap.

Everyone at the table stopped eating. Everyone, spoons or forks halfway to their lips, turned her way and stared. All of a sudden the crackle of that innocent waxed paper sounded like a rhino tromping through dry leaves.

"Jess?" said her mother. "What are you up to now? What is that?"

It was like Show & Tell. So she showed. "Peanut butter, Mom. And jelly."

Everyone laughed. Everyone except her mother, who blushed and apologized. "I'm so sorry."

"What for?" asked Jess. "It's just a sandwich."

Chapter 2

Hello, Independence

Jess, Sadie, and Maya stood together at the kitchen counter at Jess's house, passing a jar of peanut butter back and forth. Afternoon light, yellow as butter, spilled through the blinds, across the silver mixer and bowl, the sleek black espresso maker, the copper pans hanging from racks over the stove.

Sadie said, "I hope your babysitter is ten hours late, not ten minutes."

Jess said, "Don't tell my mom that."

Right on cue the phone rang. Again.

"Mom. Vicki's always late. I'll call you

the second she gets here." She set down the phone. Sadie slid the jar toward her. Maya handed her the spoon.

Mmmm, extra-crunchy. Was there anything better?

"Where is Vicki, anyway?" Maya asked.

"Don't you start." Jess reluctantly screwed the lid back on the almost-empty jar. "We should put this back before Vicki gets here. She'll say it's nasty."

"It's not nasty," said Sadie, spoon dangling from her mouth.

"It's scrumptious," said Maya. "Unhygienic, but scrumptious."

"Vicki's awful," said Jess. "She treats me like I'm three years old. Last time she tried to get me to take a nap."

Sadie opened the fridge. "Who wants orange juice?"

"Just don't spill any. Vicki goes nuts

when the counter's all sticky."

The phone buzzed. "Hi, Mom. Stop worrying. We're not going to let that homeless zombie in. Dad already called to make sure we boarded up the windows. He sounded happy. He hit a home run. He wants to talk tonight. Bye."

Jess poured herself a glass of orange juice and stood against the refrigerator, right next to the drawing of a snowman she'd made

in first grade and a picture of her dad in his Maryvale Stars uniform.

"My dad," Sadie said, "totally loves that your dad's job is playing baseball."

Jess swirled her juice. Too much pulp. "Yeah, Dad's off living his dream on the ball field two hundred miles away. Mom's living her dream at Chef Paul's restaurant ten blocks away. And I'm here living the thousand-phone-calls-a-day nightmare."

"Is your mom still mad at you?" asked Maya. "For smuggling in contraband?"

"It was a sandwich. Not a . . ." Jess groped for a word.

Maya helped her out. "Not a black mamba, one of the ten deadliest snakes in the world."

"Right."

The phone buzzed. Ugh, would she never stop? "Be me!" She thrust the phone at Sadie.

"Yes, Mom. No, Mom." Sadie sounded perfect: a little impatient, a lot annoyed. "Bye." She turned to Jess. "She knew it wasn't you. And she said you shouldn't make any more jokes about homeless people."

"I didn't say homeless *people*. I said homeless *zombies*. Parents never listen."

"Ms. M said most grown-ups see what they want to see," Sadie offered. "Probably they hear what they want to hear, too."

"That is so true," Maya agreed. "Your parents thought Ms. M's classic witch hat was some new fourth-grade fashion craze." She leaned across the counter. "Have you heard anything from her since she left? It's been, like, a month. You said that she said you guys would keep in touch."

"Yeah, any news?" Jess loved Sadie's stories about Ms. M, the witch Sadie had met while Jess and Maya were on vacation at Moosehead Lake.

"I did get a postcard from Cozumel. It either said she was at the zoo and wished me well, or she lost a shoe and caribou smell. Witches have terrible handwriting."

Maya's eyes widened. "How many witches did you meet while we were gone?"

"Just the one," Sadie said, smiling. "But she taught me a lot."

Jess glanced at the wall clock. "Vicki was supposed to

be here half an hour ago. Maybe she's not coming. How cool would that be?"

"You could prove how responsible you are," said Sadie.

"And self-reliant," said Maya. "And—"

The phone interrupted. Jess sighed. "Hi, Mom. Vicki—"

What her mother said made her stand straighter. As if she was suddenly taller. As if the house was suddenly larger.

She set down the phone, turned toward her friends, and announced, "Unbelievable. Vicki can't make it. For the next two hours, we're on our own."

The words hung in the air. ON OUR OWN. It was as if every door and window had been flung open.

"I love autonomy!" said Maya. "We can do whatever we want."

"Let's eat the rest of the peanut butter!" said Jess.

"I wonder if we shouldn't be responsible first," said Sadie as she set the glasses in the sink next to the spoon.

"Then the peanut butter?"

"We'll see." Sadie could do a Mom voice with no trouble at all. Everybody laughed.

Maya rinsed and dried the dishes. Sadie put them away. Jess wiped the counter with the blue sponge. They stood in the spotless kitchen and looked at each other.

"Let's do something noisy," Jess said.

"How about Scrabble?" said Maya.

"Scrabble is not noisy."

"It is when you lose. Remember?"

Sadie spoke quietly. "What if we cooked dinner? That would prove to your mom that you're fine on your own."

"Yes!" said Maya. "No more babysitters. Ever. Good-bye, Vicki. Hello, independence."

"Great, except for one little problem," Jess reminded her. "I can't cook."

"I've seen my dad make lasagna," Sadie persisted. She waved her hand toward a shelf under the counter. "There are about twenty cookbooks right here. Easy-peasy."

Jess remembered not so long ago when Sadie would have given in. Would have let Jess overrule her. Not anymore. Whatever magic Ms. M worked had resulted in a new Sadie. More adventurous. Less timid. More fun.

"It's a genius idea," Maya chimed in. "Your mom will completely love that you were so solicitous."

"Huh?" said Sadie and Jess as one.

"Thoughtful and considerate. The storm will pass, and she'll forget all about your disgraceful PB and J."

"I don't know . . ."

"Come on," urged Sadie. "Let's pick a cookbook and get started."

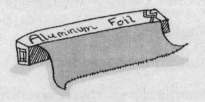

Chapter 3
This Should Work

A few minutes later, the troops were at their stations—Jess in front of the refrigerator, Maya in front of the pantry—waiting for General Sadie to call out ingredients.

"Italian sausage?"

"No."

"Ground beef?"

"Not much."

"Vegetarian, then," Sadie declared. "Maya, canned tomatoes?"

"Uh-huh. And lasagna noodles."

"Mozzarella, Jess? Any vegetables?"

"Yes on the mozzarella. For vegetables, there's onions, broccoli, spinach, and I think this other thing is a zucchini. Or a bowling pin for Shrek."

Sadie filled a pot with water for the noodles. Maya chopped some vegetables and slipped them into the microwave. Jess bunched together little leafy greens from the garden. "This whole thing makes me really nervous," she admitted.

"Relax," said Maya. "It's like a science project. All we have to do is follow the directions."

Jess opened a jar of spaghetti sauce. "Remember Science Fair last year? 'Do white candles burn faster than red candles?' And 'Is mold the same if the bread is different?'"

Maya probed the vegetables with a fork. "My favorite was 'Does magnetism affect plant growth?' Tyler Banks puts two smiley-face magnets on one pot of pumpkin seeds and nothing on the other pot of pumpkin seeds." She started to laugh. "So when pot number one grows something and number

two doesn't, he concludes that the seeds in pot number two don't have a sense of humor."

"He's a pretty good tennis player," Jess observed. "Big serve, weak backhand."

She looked around the kitchen. So far, so good. Sadie had drained the noodles without burning herself. Maya had chopped the vegetables and still had all her fingers. She had personally spilled only a little tomato sauce.

"Where are we?" asked Sadie. "I mean, what layer are we on?"

Maya squinted at the pan. "Three, I think. Just dump in all the noodles and what's left of the sauce."

Jess read from the recipe. "Bake covered at three-fifty for forty minutes." She frowned. "Covered with what? A quilt?"

"They probably mean aluminum foil or something," Sadie guessed.

Jess rummaged around in the drawer under the oven. "This should work." She pulled out a white rectangular lid. "It's the same size as the pan."

Carefully Jess slid the lasagna onto the oven's top rack, closed the door, and sighed with relief. "Now we have to wash everything

and put it right back where it was."

Sadie, who was lugging the biggest pot toward the sink, stopped in front of the window and froze. "There's a cat out there that looks like Onyx!"

"Ms. M's Onyx?" Maya hurried to peer over her shoulder. "Maybe her postcard said 'See you soon!' In Aztec!"

"Except I don't see anything." Jess leaned so close to the window that her nose touched the glass.

"He was there a second ago, I swear."

"Let's go look," Maya said.

Jess's backyard was big. Mock orange and lilac bushes grew on three sides. The girls spread out, each inspecting a different section.

"Kitty, kitty?" Sadie crooned, squatting beside the zinnias.

"Are you sure it was Onyx?" said Jess as she circled the trash cans. "Not a squirrel? Or a rock?"

"I'm sure it was a cat, and it was black."

Maya knelt next to Jess's mother's herb garden. She plucked a stem from a plant and smooshed it between her fingers. "This smells so good. Maybe it's catnip, because it's making me want to roll around on the ground."

Sadie plopped beside her. "Hey, if we can't find a cat, we could always do the cat yoga pose." She got onto her hands and knees and arched her back. "Or downward dog." She straightened her arms and legs and pushed her back end toward the sky.

Maya flipped onto her side. "Let's do comatose sloth."

All three girls sprawled on the warm grass. The scent of herbs swirled in the breeze. The late summer sun dripped down and pooled on their faces. It was so easy to let their eyes close.

Jess sat up first. Sniffed. "Do you smell that?"

"*Mmmm,*" Sadie responded, not opening her eyes.

"It smells familiar."

Now Maya was sitting, too. Suddenly she gasped. "Oh, no! Remember that time in first grade when we took the grill lighter and Jess's dolls into the garage and played—"

Sadie shot to her feet. "Volcano Barbies!"

They raced for the kitchen door, reaching

it just as the smoke detector started to blare:
Screeeeeeeee!!!!

"Open a window!" Jess yelled. Sadie plugged her nose with one hand and grabbed a potholder with the other. Maya whacked at the smoke detector with a broom handle, trying to silence it.

Minutes later, all was quiet. The smoke detector hung from the ceiling like a giant dead spider. On the stovetop sat the stinky, smoldering ruins.

"Melted cheese, melted plastic," Maya said. "Not a nutritious combination."

"Aluminum foil," Sadie whispered, shaking her head. "I said aluminum foil."

"How was I supposed to know it was the wrong lid?" Jess moaned. "It fit the pan."

"At least it was white," Maya said semi-brightly. "It kind of matches the mozzarella."

I am so dead, Jess thought.

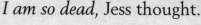

Chapter 4
The New Babysitter

"We were trying to be nice to you yesterday. We made one little mistake. One!"

Jess's mother, already in her white chef's jacket, continued transferring items—checkbook, wallet, keys—from one purse to another. She took a sip of coffee. "I appreciate the thought. I really do. And I'm sure someday my oven won't smell like a tire factory every time I turn it on."

"I'll wipe it out with soap and water again. I promise."

"Honey." Her mother sighed. "It's a big deal for me to work with Chef Paul, even for a week. The truth is, I don't want to waste any more of that time worrying. You need a reliable babysitter. Someone who can keep you out of trouble and make sure you eat healthy meals."

"Peanut butter has protein and fiber and a whole bunch of other stuff."

"Discussion over, Jess."

Jess held on to her mother's wrists with both hands. "Sadie's dad makes super-healthy smoothies. Let me stay over there today. I'll even drink the green ones."

"I said, discussion over."

"Vicki is boring, but at least I know her," Jess grumbled.

"This babysitter is highly recommended. She has a background in nutrition."

"So she has sprouts growing out of her ears?"

Just then the doorbell rang. Her mother picked up her purse and chef's knife bag and hurried down the hall to answer it.

Jess looked past her. Or tried to. She heard hellos, but she couldn't see anyone.

Then her mother stepped aside and there stood the new babysitter. In a KISS THE COOK sweatshirt. And a pointy hat.

"Jess," her mother said. "Meet Ms. M."

Out came the witch's small hand. Her eyes flashed, alert and inviting.

Jess could only stare.

Here, right in her living room, was Ms. M. Sadie's Ms. M.

Just as Sadie had described her, including the hat. Especially the hat.

Did Mom know she'd hired a witch as a babysitter?

"So, Ms. M," her mother said. "We had a long chat on the phone yesterday. You've got my cell number. Anything you need to ask before I go?"

"Everything's peachy," said the witch. "You run along. We'll be fine, won't we, Jess."

Too overwhelmed to speak, Jess nodded. Her mother kissed her on the forehead and said, "Today you may not call your friends. You may not leave the house. We'll see about tomorrow."

"Why don't I just tie her to a chair," said the witch.

Jess's mother turned slightly, looking puzzled. "Of course you care. I just told Jess you came highly recommended."

As the car backed down the driveway, the witch said, "Let's wave." So they did.

Once they'd closed the door, Jess asked, "You aren't really going to tie me to a chair, are you?"

"I was only having a bit of fun," Ms. M assured her, collapsing onto the couch.

"So it's really you?"

"Back from Mexico. I was investigating an Ethel sighting."

"Sadie told us about Ethel. How she turned . . ."

"Into a bird. Yes. A yellow warbler. *Setophaga petechia*."

Jess began, "Because a spell . . ."

Ms. M nodded and her hat wobbled. "Yes. A spell that did not turn out well at all."

So it was true, what Sadie had told them about Ms. M and Ethel. Not that they hadn't believed her. Well, they'd wanted to believe her. But now Jess *really* believed her. Really and truly.

Jess asked, "Did you find Ethel?"

The witch shook her head. "Alas, no. Some excellent enchiladas, but no Ethel." She sifted through the small pile of magazines on the coffee table. Held up *Bon Appétit*. Sighed.

"Ethel subscribed to this one. And of course to *The Enchanted Epicure*."

Jess perched on the arm of the couch. "Does Sadie know you're back? She talks about you all the time."

"And I talk about her. But at present, I am here to see you."

"I can't wait to tell her!" She reached for the phone and then stopped. "You're not going to tell Mom, are you?"

"That you called a friend even though you're not supposed to? You haven't actually called yet."

Jess hit Sadie's number. "You're not the boss of me."

"I'm sure I'm not."

"How did you even get this job?" Ugh, the

call was taking forever to go through! She hung up and tried again.

"You heard your mother." Ms. M leaped to her feet. Straightened her hat. "I always come highly recommended."

Chapter 5

Mortar and Pestle

In the kitchen, Ms. M walked around the butcher block island, caressed the mixer, admired the knives.

Jess stared at the phone. "It's weird," she said. "There's just this crackly sound."

"Let me listen." Ms. M tilted her hat to one side so she could get the phone closer to her ear. She said, "*Mishkabobnorbiddldom-nexiamanmus.*"

"What was that?" asked Jess.

"Gibberish," replied the witch. "Most gadgets speak it. I used it to reason with a surly toaster the other day, but this phone doesn't seem in the mood to communicate."

She picked up a small bowl next to the stove. Resting inside the bowl was something that looked like a little baseball bat. "Now here's an item that speaks volumes. A mortar and pestle. Electric gadgets are fine in their place, but this has gravitas. It's got history."

Beaming, she held out the little bat for Jess to examine. "Look. Look how worn the pestle is. Who knows how many hands have used it, to make how many meals."

"I think Mom uses it to mash garlic." Jess made a face. "Ick."

The witch nodded sagely. "Nothing like a mortar and pestle for grinding spices and herbs. And Baba Yaga flies around in one. Hers is much roomier than this beauty, of course."

"Who is Baba Yaga?"

"A friend of mine from the Old Country. I'll tell you about her another time."

Ms. M flipped the faucet on and off. Opened and closed drawers. Eyed the pots of herbs on the windowsill. "Did you know,"

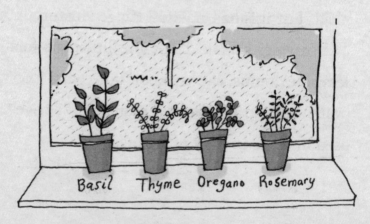

Basil   Thyme   Oregano   Rosemary

she said after a while, "that kitchens didn't used to be in the house? They were off by themselves. Because they were hot and stinky and caught fire a lot."

"Thanks for the reminder."

"Even the best chefs make mistakes," said the witch, peering into the bread box. "You heard what happened to Ethel. And she was a champion baker. Her Toad House cookies took the blue ribbon every year at the Wisconsin State Fair. Except for back in 1992, when she accidentally used iguana extract instead of toad. The iguana-intolerant judge swelled up like a water buffalo." The witch clucked her tongue. "It was weeks before he could stop wallowing in the nearest mudhole."

"I don't have to worry about that," Jess said sourly. "I have you here to make sure I eat all the *right* foods. The *nutritious* foods—"

A plaintive meow outside the open window interrupted her. "Hey! That really was Onyx in the backyard yesterday!"

"He's usually close by." Ms. M rubbed her hands together. "Want to shoot some hoops in the driveway?"

"Are you serious?"

"I can't drive the lane like I used to, but we could play HORSE. Or I'll stand under the basket and feed you the ball."

"Don't you want to watch birds, like you did with Sadie?"

"Are you Sadie?"

"No, but . . ."

"So, are we going to play or not?"

Chapter 6
Good Game

Outside, a cheering section of cicadas droned from the trees. Jess did jumping jacks to warm up. Ms. M bounced the ball a few times. She swayed in front of Jess, muttering, "Insy-outsy, alley-oop, make the ball go through the hoop."

"This isn't going to be fair," Jess protested.

"Good point. You're taller than I am. You're a lot younger, and you've played a lot more round ball than I have. You should at least spot me the H in HORSE."

"No, I mean it's not going to be fair to *me*. You're a witch."

Ms. M waved that away. "Among other things. I'm also somebody who doesn't like to sit around and appreciates fresh air."

"Somebody wearing a black pointy hat and pointy shoes."

"To make me look taller. And black is slimming. Everybody knows that. All right, shall we get started?"

Jess made a simple lay-up. The witch did, too. Jess shot from way outside. So did the witch. Jess tried a little scoop shot. The witch answered, though the ball did circle the rim before it dropped.

"Lucky," said Jess.

"Practice. A bunch of us get together in Phoenix every July for the Coven in the Oven. After the meetings we play round ball and swim."

"You don't wear those hats in the pool, do you?"

"In the pool? Of course not, silly. But we take all the black cats in."

Jess stared.

"Kidding. Just making sure you were paying attention."

The witch retrieved the basketball

and held it as she gazed around. "What a beautiful herb garden. Look at the variety. Amiable rosemary, enigmatic thyme. Oh, and there's dill. Ethel's favorite. She always said that without dill a pickle would just be a cucumber."

Jess walked closer to Ms. M. "Which one is dill, again?"

The witch pointed to each herb and repeated its name. "I love how rosemary looks like a little forest. And it's essential for memory spells. I always keep some handy for when I've misplaced my car keys."

"You have a car?"

"When I can find it." The witch tossed her the ball. "Your shot."

They played on, with the witch missing a few while Jess missed only one or two. The game was at HORS when Ms. M stopped to rest. She was panting a little.

"Are you okay?" Jess asked.

Ms. M straightened her shoulders. She spun the ball on her finger like a globe. "Get your popcorn ready, 'cause I'm gonna put on a show!"

She sank hook shots from both sides. She

dribbled almost to the end of the driveway and sank one from downtown. Finally, she turned her back to Jess and made the last shot without even looking.

"Wow, good game," said Jess. She held up her hand for a high five.

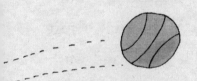

"A little lower, please, dear. My shoulder's sore."

"Want to play again?"

"Maybe later. Right now let's go inside and see what we can find for lunch."

Lunch. So *that* was Ms. M's plan. Wear Jess out. Get her hungry enough so she'd gobble up whatever disgusting muck dropped onto her plate. Well. They'd just see about that. "Okay. I'll go up and wash my hands first."

Alone in her room, Jess tried to call Sadie again. Gibberish. Hmmmm. Then she actually did wash her hands. She thumped downstairs ready to sneer at anything stewed, poached, blanched, slow-roasted, or fricasseed.

But wait. What was that in the center of the table? It looked like a can of tuna, without the can but still shaped like it, on top of a lettuce leaf.

"Hope you like tuna salad!" Ms. M sang out.

"That's not tuna salad. Tuna salad has celery and herbs and mayonnaise all mixed together." Jess shuddered.

The witch pointed at the tuna, then the lettuce. "Tuna plus salad equals tuna salad."

"That isn't how my mom would make it. Not that I want that."

"Is your mom, as you say, the boss of me?"

"Um, yeah. Technically."

"True." The witch lifted her hat and scratched her head. "Well, if you'd prefer

your traditional family recipe." She moved to take away the plate.

"No! This is fine." It didn't look that bad, actually. It looked honest. No mystery ingredients. No weird seasonings.

On the other side of the table the witch pulled out a chair and climbed into it. She handed Jess a fork. "Dig in, dear."

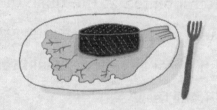

Chapter 7
Boogers Begone

That night Jess was watching a baseball game on TV when her mother came into the living room and sat beside her.

"Did you and Ms. M actually eat three cans of tuna and a whole head of lettuce?"

"Mom, tuna plus lettuce equals tuna salad."

Her mother frowned. Took a deep breath.

"She is the oddest little person, isn't she?"

"She's really different," Jess admitted. "But we had fun. She's not like Vicki, who just lies around texting. Ms. M knows a lot about herbs and stuff. She loves your garden."

"I'm glad." Her mother seemed about to say something else, but Jess locked her gaze on the screen. Bottom of the ninth, two players on base, two out. Clutch time. The batter sent a weak pop-up down the third-base line, easily snagged by the left fielder. Jess groaned. "Dad would never choke like that!"

Her mother laughed. "Because he knows you'd make him run wind sprints if he did."

Jess leaned sideways and let her mother stroke her hair. "I miss him."

"He'll be home soon."

"You don't think they'll make the playoffs?"

Her mother laughed again. "C'mon, Coach. Bedtime." Wriggling out from under Jess, she rose to her feet and held out her hands. Jess clasped them and let herself be pulled from the couch to her bedroom.

While Jess arranged the covers just the way she liked them, her mother wandered the room, scooping up dirty clothes, returning stray stuffed animals to their shelf. She stooped to kiss her daughter's forehead and then lingered in the doorway for a moment. "I'm glad you had fun today, sweetheart. Tomorrow have fun while eating something besides tuna, okay?" She closed the door.

Instantly Jess's cozy feeling drained away and left behind itchy, uncomfortable thoughts. No matter what she ate, no matter what she did, in her mother's eyes it would always be wrong. *She* would always be wrong.

Tap, tap.

What was that?

Tap, tap, tap.

It was coming from the window. Something was out there. Or someone. Someone in a tall black hat!

She leaped out of bed and pushed open the window to find Ms. M and Onyx hunched together on the roof. Clouds ghosted through the sky behind them, passing over a pale sliver of moon.

"How did you get up here?" Jess asked, incredulous.

"How do witches get anywhere?"

"On a broomstick?"

"Don't be silly. Do you know what that would do to my hair? Anyway, how we got up here isn't nearly as important as why. Sadie's parents are still trying to sell the playhouse, so Onyx and I need a place to spend the night. I was wondering if we could sleep on that comfortable couch in your family room. May we come all the way in? I feel a bit conspicuous."

Jess stepped back as Ms. M, holding Onyx, climbed over the sill. Once inside, the cat squirmed out of the witch's arms, bounded up on the bed, and disappeared under the covers.

"I'd love for you to stay here," Jess whispered. "But my mom's got terrible allergies. That's why we don't have any pets."

"Oh, I can take care of that. It's just for one night. Two at the most. Then I can stay with a witch I know. She has a couple of little ones visiting her now, and you know how cramped gingerbread cottages can be. But she assures me that the kids will be gone soon."

Jess gulped. "She's going to eat them?"

"That's certainly one way to stop them tracking dirt all over her carpets. Though I believe the plan is for her to put them on a plane back to Cleveland. They're her grandchildren." Ms. M yawned and scratched her beaky nose. "I promise we'll be out before your mother is awake. Then I'll be at the front door at eight sharp. She'll never even know we were here."

Jess took a deep breath, like she did before the kick-off in a big game. "Okay."

The witch dragged a reluctant Onyx from his hiding place, scooped him up, and disappeared out the door. Back in bed, Jess mentally recited soccer player names to relax.

Abby Wambach, Alex Morgan, Megan Rapinoe …
She was just drifting off when a sharp, all-too-familiar smell jolted her awake.

Smoke? Oh, no, not again!

Creeping past her parents' bedroom, she listened for movement inside but, miraculously, heard none. Once she reached the stairs, she broke into a run.

Sure enough, a flickering light leaked out from under the family room door, and the burning smell was unmistakable.

She didn't bother to knock. "What are you doing? You can't build a fire in here!"

Without looking up from her cauldron, which bubbled energetically beside the computer desk, Ms. M said, "Do you want your mother to wake up with red eyes and a runny nose?"

"Do you want her to wake up with her pajamas on fire?"

"Oh, this isn't a real fire. It's an illusion. Like when so-called magicians make elephants disappear."

"So why am I about to die of heatstroke?" Jess fanned her face.

"It's an excellent illusion. Trust me." The witch held her hat in place with one hand, leaned over the cauldron, and sniffed. "Your mother will be fit as a fiddle in the morning."

"Mom's never going to drink that."

"She doesn't have to drink it. It's aromatherapy. For

nasal congestion. It's called Boogers Begone."

"Yuck." Jess took a step back, covering her nose with her hand. "It smells worse than the lasagna that got me in all that trouble."

"Those are the allergen blockers."

"Could you at least put out the fire?"

"What fire?"

It was true. Only the battered cauldron sat at the witch's feet, no smoke or flames in sight. On top of the couch a croissant-shaped Onyx tucked his head under his front paws.

"Go to sleep, dear. Big day tomorrow."

"Why?" asked Jess, suspicious. "What's going to happen?"

"I don't know. I like to think that every day's a big day. Tomorrow especially, since we get to spend it together."

As Ms. M settled herself beneath a red-plaid fleece throw, Jess looked around the family room. At her soccer trophies. At the framed photo of Mom from chef school graduation. At Dad's autographed baseball.

"My dad's been gone a long time," Jess blurted. "I really miss him."

"Gone a long time," repeated the witch. "I certainly know about that." With a sigh, she asked, "Would you mind turning off the light on your way out?"

The witch's breathing sounded slow and steady. It seemed she had fallen asleep in an instant.

Jess flipped the switch. *Click*. Darkness swallowed the room.

Ms. M's voice floated through the thick

shadows. "I like to think that Ethel is happy, wherever she is. But I miss her. I miss her with my whole heart and soul." A soft rustling of fabric came from the couch, as if the witch were turning over. "Sweet dreams, dear."

"You too, Ms. M."

It was colder out in the hallway, and Jess shivered a little as she tiptoed back up to her room. She had almost made it when a noise stopped her. A loud sneeze, and then the honk of her mother blowing her nose.

Terrific.

Chapter 8
Fra Foow

The next morning Jess made sure to get downstairs first. Heart thumping in her ears, she opened the door to the family room.

No witch. No cat. No cauldron.

The fleece throw lay folded neatly at the end of the couch.

Whew.

She was in the kitchen, pouring herself a glass of juice, when her mother walked in, already dressed for work.

"I thought for sure I was coming down with something last night. Sneezing, sore throat, runny nose. You name it. But I feel great this morning." Her mother hovered behind her. "Want me to fix you an omelet before I go? I brought home some wonderful leeks from Chef Paul's yesterday."

"I don't want a leaky omelet."

"You know leeks are relatives of onions. Last I checked, you liked onions."

"That's okay. I'll eat when Ms. M gets here."

"Honey—" her mother began, but right then, as if Jess had conjured it, the doorbell rang.

Jess popped a slice of bread in the toaster and listened to the voices in the hall.

"Seriously, Ms. M," her mother said as the two women entered the kitchen. "Jess is not an orca. Three cans of tuna is too much."

"I understand. Goat bran and beet germ for today's menu."

"Good," her mother said with a slightly bewildered expression. "That's a start."

"Are those even real foods?" Jess asked once her mother had gone. With a knife she dug out a thick gob of peanut butter and spread it over the toast.

"Every balanced diet includes imaginary foods. For vim." The witch rubbed her hands together in that let's-get-down-to-business way. "But right now we should decide how to spend our day. I'd like to get outdoors again. How does tennis sound?"

"It sounds great, but—"

"Of course I'll need a white cable-knit sweater," the witch interrupted. "To get into the true spirit of the game. One with a black stripe at the neck. Do you have one?"

"I think Dad does, but it'll be too big."

"Maybe a little. I don't mind. Run and fetch it, please, while I cut up some veggies."

A few minutes later Jess handed Ms. M her father's sweater. She watched with growing alarm as Ms. M slipped it on. It hung almost to the witch's shoes.

Ms. M took a couple of practice swings with a stalk of celery. She admired her outfit in the chrome of the toaster. "I've always been a trendsetter. In the fall, I think you'll see this look everywhere."

"On Mars," Jess muttered to herself. Then, louder, "Maybe a different hat? A visor?"

"Oh, no. My hat is perfect. Black cuts the glare like nobody's business. Find us a couple of racquets and let's hit the courts!

I'll bring these vegetables for a snack."

"Peanut butter, too?"

"Of course. Just drop it in my bag."

As they made their way toward the park, Jess couldn't believe more people didn't stare. Those who did seemed amused, but not in a mean way. Mrs. Timley stopped raking as they passed her yard and called out, "A beautiful day for a game! Have fun!" A teenage boy whizzing by on a skateboard gave them a thumbs-up.

Jess twirled her racket as she walked. "Are you as good at tennis as you are at basketball?"

"Sometimes better."

They stopped in front of the Gladstones', a large house with a curving walkway. Bushes heavy with pink roses nodded agreeably.

They each bent toward a different blossom and sniffed.

"Lovely," said Ms. M.

"We used to have roses in our yard," Jess said. "But they caught some kind of disease, so Dad got rid of them."

"Roses do require a lot of care." The witch pulled off a single pink petal and rubbed it against her cheek. "Special food. Fungicide. Pruning. Some gardeners think they're worth all that trouble, but I prefer more independent plants. Mint, for instance. Just as fragrant as any rose, and it grows like, well, like what many people think it is—a weed."

A large yellow dog came loping around the side of the Gladstones' garage and headed toward them, tongue flopping.

Jess tensed but stood her ground. "That's Toby. He's kind of a drool monster."

"Oh, he's all right." Ms. M stepped forward. "Anyway, I speak Dog." She patted Toby's shaggy head. "*Fra fra*," she said. "*Foow*."

Toby sat back on his haunches and barked.

"Why, thank you," the witch responded. She beamed at Jess. "He likes my sweater."

"*Fra, fra?*" Jess repeated.

"It's *arf, arf* backward. Now you can speak Dog, too."

"You're joking."

"Try it," the witch urged.

"*Arf*," said Jess softly.

Toby stared.

"That was English," said the witch. "Try again."

Jess cleared her throat. "*Fra, fra. Foow.*"

The dog's ears went up. He pressed his heavy, clumsy paws against Jess's chest and tried to lick her face.

"Down, Toby!"

"You just told him he was handsome but smelly."

"No, I didn't. I said '*Fra, fra*' just like you did."

"It's all in the intonation, dear. Like Chinese. It's not your fault. Learning a second language takes practice."

"So if I insulted him, why did he act all happy?"

"'Smelly' may be an insult to you, dear, but dogs live by their noses. To him, 'smelly' is high praise." Ms. M continued.

"You're welcome, Toby. *Fra fra fra fra*."

The dog's thick tail wagged against Jess's knees.

"Toby!" Mrs. Gladstone's voice rang out from the backyard. He took one last, friendly look at them and galloped back the way he'd come.

"*Foow*!" Ms. M called. Then, to Jess, "I told him we'd be in touch."

Chapter 9
The Boss of the Sun

Jess and Ms. M turned a corner. The park was only half a block away, but they couldn't see the court yet. Trees dappled the sun-baked sidewalk with huge, cooling shadows. A dozen small birds scattered out of their path in a dozen different directions.

"Excuse us," Ms. M called after them.

"What kind of birds are those? I bet Sadie would know."

"House wrens. *Troglodytes aedon*, if you want to be formal."

"Do you know everything's name?"

The witch stopped to think. "Not all, but a lot. My mother and I were seriously rural. We grew a lot of our own food."

"Sometimes I help Mom in the garden," Jess admitted. "She never gets mad at me when we're outside picking tomatoes. Inside, when she's pouring balsamic vinegar all over them and shoving them in my face? That's a different story." She almost gagged at the memory of a thick tomato slice drenched in brown liquid. Like a red sponge in a muddy puddle.

"Italians used to call tomatoes *pomi d'oro*." When Jess looked at her blankly, the witch translated. "Apples of gold. Isn't that lovely?"

"They could call them fudge donuts. I still wouldn't eat them raw."

Ms. M nodded hello to a beagle trotting by on a yellow leash. At the other end of the leash, a middle-aged man struggled to keep up.

The witch turned back to Jess. "You're a strong young woman. I like that. You stand by your convictions."

"Too bad Mom doesn't see it that way. She wishes I was still a baby so she could cram food in my mouth."

"How do you know?" Ms. M asked.

"I just do."

"Interesting."

"What?"

"I didn't realize they taught mind reading in the public schools."

Before Jess could think of a snappy response, the witch tugged at Jess's hand and said, "I feel like kicking up my heels. Let's skip the rest of the way!"

Even before they reached the court, Jess heard the *thwock thwock* of tennis balls. How annoying. "We'll have to wait," she said. "Someone else is playing."

"That's all right. We have plenty of time."

Two boys who looked a few years older than Jess lazily hit the ball back and forth. Sometimes. Mostly they played air guitar with their racquets.

"Dunanaduwawodunananananananatata,"

the taller one sang, sinking to his knees for a solo.

"When will you guys be done?" Jess called out.

They glared at her. "When we're done, weirdos," answered the shorter boy. His friend jumped to his feet and pretended to smash his "guitar" against the court like a punk rocker.

Jess and Ms. M sat on a splintery bench, dangling their feet. "Boys are so stupid," Jess said.

"They're just novices," said Ms. M.

Jess thought she knew what that word

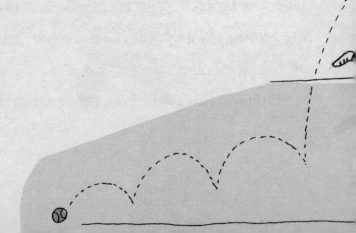

meant—beginners. She'd heard Maya use it before. "Then they shouldn't hog the court when people who actually know how to play are waiting."

"Not novices at tennis," the witch corrected. "They're novices at being boys. At pretty much everything, actually."

"Dude!" the shorter boy shouted. "Watch

this!" He ran at the net and tried to hurdle it, but caught his foot in the mesh. Giggling, he sprawled across the center of the net—half on one side, half on the other—while his friend hurled tennis balls at his back.

Jess sighed. "Were boys like that when you were my age?"

"Oh, yes. My brothers used to dare each other to eat guppies. They'd climb trees and fall out of them. My mother told me more than once she was so happy when the midwife told her I was a girl."

"How many brothers do you have?"

"Three. Two older and one younger."

"Are they witches, too?"

"They run a small business together. Ever see the commercials for Wizard Deodorant?

'Odor disappears like magic'? That's them. I'll let you in on a secret—it really *is* magic. That and lavender oil."

Now the boys were playing catch with three balls, attempting to keep them all in the air at the same time like jugglers. And failing miserably. And cracking up.

"Seriously?" said Jess loud enough for them to hear.

"Fine, fine," the shorter boy said. "We'll play." He looked across the net at his friend. "Forty love, right?" He smirked at Jess. "In the first game of a three-set match. Which could take hours."

Jess turned to Ms. M. "There's another court about ten blocks away."

"Let's wait another minute." Ms. M

narrowed her eyes and hummed a low, almost guttural tune.

"What are you doing?" Jess asked.

"If their racquets melted, they'd have to go home."

"Cool. Melt their shoes, too."

Jess watched intently as the tall boy bounced the ball a few times. He squinted, held up his hand for shade, squinted again. "The sun is really intense, man. Switch sides, okay?"

"Then I can't see."

"But I'm serving."

"So?"

"C'mon, I can't even see the net."

As they passed each other, they pretended to fence with their racquets. Then they took their places.

"Dude, I'm burning up."

The tall boy grimaced. "It's even worse over here."

Ms. M hopped off the bench. "So, may my friend and I play?"

"Lots of luck," the tall boy said as he and his friend stumbled off the court.

The witch tossed a ball into the air and unleashed a blistering serve. "Seems fine to me."

"How did you do that?" Jess asked after the boys had gone.

"It's all in the wrist." Ms. M beamed and twirled her racquet.

"Not the serve. The sun. How did you make it so hot?"

"Oh, I'm not the boss of the sun, dear.

The sun has a mind of its own." The witch crouched, racquet outstretched, and shifted her weight from foot to foot. "Now are you going to ask questions or serve?"

Chapter 10

Transylvanian Tofu

Forty-five minutes later, Jess jogged up to the net and extended one hand. "Now we're even. You beat me at basketball, I beat you at tennis. But it was close. You had me at forty-thirty a lot."

"I'm nimble, if I do say so myself. I'm seriously considering joining the Cheerful

Crones' Lawn and Tennis Club when I get back home."

They relaxed on a park bench beside the bike trail. Jess wiped off the handles of the racquets with a white towel. Ms. M dug two water bottles out of her black bag and handed Jess one.

"Hungry now?" asked the witch.

"Definitely," said Jess.

"I'm thinking armadillo hash with Thai peanut sauce. Except, armadillo isn't in season this time of year, so"—she reached into the bag—"I have this."

Jess inspected the little carton. "Tofu. *Blech*."

"But this is Transylvanian tofu. You can't get it in the U.S. It's very tasty."

armadillo

hash?

"Can't we just have peanut butter sandwiches?"

"We'll use peanut butter in the sauce."

Sauce. The word gave Jess the willies. She was not a fan of sauce. Especially slathered all over something that looked and probably tasted like a rat's mattress.

The witch continued taking items out of her bag, identifying them as she went. "Coconut milk. Curry paste. Lime."

"Paste. Is that to glue the coconut milk to the lime?"

"I am going to combine them." She surveyed the park. "Let's see. We need a grill. The sauce has to be reduced slightly to concentrate the flavor."

Jess pointed to the witch's black bag.

"Please tell me you don't have charcoal in there, too."

"Not at the moment. But there's every chance those people who were grilling hot dogs earlier left some embers."

"I sure hope not."

Ms. M led the way toward a cluster of picnic tables. She put her things down on the nearest one and held her hand over the grate on the grill. "Lucky us. Will you find the ginger root, garlic, and cilantro in my bag, please? And while you're in there, see if you don't run into my mortar and pestle."

"That thing of my mom's you showed me yesterday?"

"Like that, but smaller. Traveling size."

Jess opened the worn black bag and

peered inside. She opened it wider. Then wider still. No matter how wide the opening got, there was nothing but darkness. "I can't see anything."

"Sorry, I packed the Transylvanian tofu in night to keep it fresh. The darkness will evaporate eventually. Just feel around if you don't want to wait."

Jess touched something soft. Something soft that squeaked. She yanked her hand out really fast. "What was that?"

"Probably just a bat left over from . . . Well, never mind. Here." She pulled the bag toward her. "Let me." Out came the bowl-shaped mortar with ginger, garlic, and cilantro nestled inside.

"The cilantro is fresh from your mother's garden. Would you like to work with that or grill the tofu?"

"I would rather eat my tennis racquet."

Ms. M acted as if Jess hadn't said a word. "I'll mince a few things and then you can grind them a bit."

Using the cleanest part of the picnic table, the witch chopped and minced efficiently. She swept the pieces into the mortar, which she handed to Jess along with the pestle. "Introduce the ingredients to each other gently," Ms. M advised.

"What?"

"Don't pound too hard."

With the fatter, rounded end of the pestle, Jess rhythmically mashed the contents of the bowl. *Ba-dum, ba-dum, ba-dum.* As she worked, the air around her began to smell like another country. Somewhere tropical and kind of mysterious.

Ms. M stopped slicing tofu and inhaled. "I love the combination of ginger and garlic," she said. "So pungent and intriguing."

"You sound like my mom."

"Tart, savory, umami," said the witch. "Smoky, peppery, luscious. Cooking is a whole other language, isn't it?"

"Like Dog."

Ms. M laughed. "With a bigger vocabulary."

She set the tofu slices on the grill, reached into her bag again, and came up with a small cauldron, about the size of a soccer ball. "Let's put your ingredients in here. We'll add the coconut milk, the peanut butter, and those veggies I chopped earlier and let it all cook for just a minute."

"Where did you get that little thing?"

The witch looked at the cauldron and frowned. "Probably some supernatural foods store." Then her face brightened. "Oh, now I remember. Ethel and I picked it up at an outdoor market in Costa Rica."

"Are you going to keep looking for Ethel?"

"Of course. I've been getting messages about her lately."

Jess peered down into the cauldron. The

soupy mixture *blurp*ed back at her. "Messages from who?"

"From everywhere. The air is always full of messages. Most people are too busy to pay attention."

The witch took two slices of tofu off the grill, slipped them onto a paper plate, and placed it on the table in front of Jess.

"One piece is really enough," she said. "More than enough."

"Wait and see," the witch said, spooning peanut sauce onto the plate.

Jess regarded her lunch with dismay. "Are you *sure* there's no tuna in your bag?"

"Go ahead. It's delicious."

Jess cut off a tiny corner of the tofu with a plastic fork, brought it slowly to her mouth, hesitated, then closed her eyes and chewed.

"Wow." Her eyes flew open. "This is amazing."

The witch grinned as she helped herself, then sat beside Jess. "I'm glad you like it."

Chapter 11
The Secrets of Sorcery

Later, after they'd been home from the park for a while, Ms. M put down her glass of iced tea and said, "I saw a dart board in your family room. Shall we play?"

Jess got to her feet. "Grab a spoon," she said. "Cause you're about to taste defeat."

Moments later Ms. M flexed all ten

fingers. "I want to warn you," she said. "I have a wicked wrist snap."

"Oh," Jess said, "now I'm scared."

The witch stepped up to the invisible line. Held her darts close to her face. Caressed their little wings. Whispered something Jess couldn't hear. Then she threw. *Whoosh! Whoosh! Whoosh!* Three darts clustered near the bull's-eye.

"That was so not fair," Jess grumbled.

"Why?"

"Because you used magic words again."

"One magic word," Ms. M corrected, swinging her arms back and forth, as if stretching. "But you're absolutely right. I don't want to have an advantage. I like facing a formidable opponent. So let me reveal to you one of the secrets of sorcery."

Jess stepped up to the invisible line. Held her darts close to her face. Caressed their little wings. Looked at Ms. M.

"Please," said the witch.

"Please what?"

"*Please* is the magic word."

Jess laughed. "You sound like my mom."

"Really?" Ms. M studied Jess with a thoughtful expression. "Then your mother must have told you that, for someone with your athleticism, *pretty please* can be even more effective." She mimed a throw. "Gives you that little extra zing in the air."

"If you say so." Jess took aim. "Pretty

please." *Whoosh!* "Pretty please." *Whoosh!* "Pretty please." *Whoosh!*

Dead center! Her darts had even knocked two of Ms. M's darts to the ground. The witch scurried over to retrieve them. "Thank you," she murmured as she bent down. Then another "thank you" as she plucked her third dart from the board.

"Is that part of the spell, too?"

"What spell? It's just good manners." The witch set her darts on the little square table next to the couch. She held her sleeve in front of her mouth to cover a yawn. "So much exercise for one day! I'm going to sleep like a sea otter tonight. Maybe better." She patted the fat arm of the sofa. "Since your couch is much more comfortable than a bed of kelp, and I won't be on my back holding a clam."

"I guess it's okay for you guys to stay here again." Jess hesitated. "But—"

"Just for one more night," Ms. M assured her. "I talked to my friend, and her grandchildren are on that plane to Cleveland early tomorrow." The witch gestured toward the window. "Leave that unlocked, and Onyx and I won't even have to disturb you. We'll slip right in."

"But my mom—"

"Yes. Here's your mother now."

Jess peered through the blinds. "I don't think so."

Humming, Ms. M put the darts back in their aluminum case and handed it to Jess as the front door opened.

"How did you do that?"

"Your mother said she'd be home about six." The witch pointed to the clock. "It's about six. Let's go say hi."

They found her mother in the entryway, clutching a white paper bag. Jess wrapped her arms around her. The bag crinkled between them. Jess breathed in deeply. "You smell like an onion. But in a good way. What's in the bag?"

"Something for dinner." Her mother rested

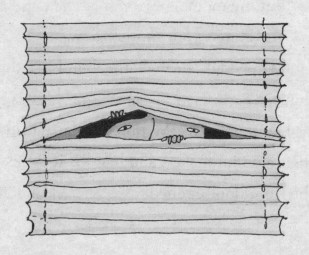

her chin on top of Jess's head. "Everything go okay today?" she said, addressing Ms. M.

"More than okay," said the witch.

Jess stepped back. "Ms. M is the best babysitter ever. Not that I need one."

The witch nodded. "You did fight off that ravenous wolf pack all by yourself."

"Oh, that's nice," said Jess's mother as she hung her slightly stained white chef's jacket on the brass hook by the door. "I'm glad you two had fun. Come into the kitchen and tell me about it. Would you like a cup of tea, Ms. M?"

"Do you have decaf?" She raised her eyebrows at Jess. "We don't want me up all night."

In the kitchen doorway, Ms. M and Jess

played no-no-you-go-first, laughing and trying to squeeze through at the same time. They settled next to each other on stools at the counter.

Jess's mother filled the kettle, stared into the empty sink, and frowned. Placing the kettle on the stove, she opened the dishwasher and shook her head. "There are no dirty dishes. Did you feed my daughter anything?"

"She's right here," Ms. M said gently. "Why don't you ask her?"

"We had a picnic at the park and"—Jess paused for dramatic effect—"I ate tofu."

"With peanut sauce," Ms. M added.

"Well. I'm amazed. Truly." The teakettle began to whistle. Jess's mother ignored it at first and then, as if suddenly waking from a trance, reached over and clicked off the burner. "I almost forgot, Chef Paul gave me the day off tomorrow to do a catering job. I'll be at home baking. So let me pay you for today, Ms. M, and then we'll see you again on Friday."

"If you don't mind, could you wait and pay me then? I love abundance."

"Of course." Jess's mother opened the

cabinet next to the refrigerator. "Let's see, I have chamomile or lemon ginger or peppermint. Which would you like?"

"They all sound wonderful, but I really should be going." Ms. M hopped down from her stool. "It's getting late. Jess, walk me to the door?"

On their way out of the kitchen, Jess glanced over her shoulder. She whispered, "Could I come down later and say good night?"

The witch put her small, warm hand over Jess's. "I would love that. I have to pick up Onyx from day care at Gato Cielo and then feed him dinner. We should be back before you're asleep."

"Cat day care?"

"He especially loves the Cabana Veranda. There's a Robodog out there that he and his friends can torment. And he has his own cushion if he wants to nap." Ms. M adjusted her hat. "The day care provider came highly recommended."

The door seemed to open itself. Ms. M tottered down the walk a few yards. Jess looked away for a moment when she heard the scrape of a kitchen chair, and by the time she looked back Ms. M was gone.

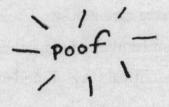

Chapter 12
Oozy and Blobby

Jess giggled as she pulled herself back onto her stool. She imagined Onyx at day care, learning how to share his yarn balls and taking turns at the scratching post.

"What's so funny?" Her mother chopped carrots into identical sticks. Lined up together, they looked like a tiny orange fence.

"Just something Ms. M said."

Dust specks chased each other lazily through the stream of evening sun flowing in from the window. The knife played a *smack-smack* rhythm against the cutting board. Jess stretched her arms over her head. They felt a little stiff. A little sore. A lot nice. This was almost the best part of playing sports, the happy-tired feeling afterward.

"I'm glad Ms. M is getting you to be more adventurous," her mother said, piling carrot sticks on Jess's favorite blue plate. "I don't know how many tofu dishes I've made for you and your dad. You wouldn't touch them."

"Mom, Ms. M's was good!"

Her mother turned away to put a plastic container in the microwave. "Mine were good, too. If you'd tried them, you'd know that."

How did this always happen? One minute her mother was glad she ate tofu. The next minute she was scolding her for not devouring tofu every day of her life. On the court Jess could drive to the basket and sink lay-up after lay-up. But here in the kitchen with her mother? Nothing but air balls.

Whatever was cooking in the microwave

began to smell . . . suspicious. The timer dinged. Her mother took out the container and lifted the lid. Steam rose like mist in a graveyard. "Are you hungry? This mac and cheese from Chef Paul's is amazing."

It didn't look amazing. It looked oozy. It looked blobby. And the smell? Like the inside of her high-tops when she forgot to wear socks.

"The truffle oil is delicious, I promise." Her mother dug a big wooden spoon into the glop.

Jess had to move fast! She pulled her plate away. "Aren't truffles those mushrooms pigs dig up in the forest? I remember when you told me that instead of reading *Goodnight Moon*. No, thanks."

Her mother sighed. "You can't just eat carrots. What about—"

"Really, I'm still full from lunch. I'll have some cereal later, maybe."

Jess retreated to the couch with her carrots. Arranged them into a fence again. A fence with her on one side and her mom on the other.

As she crunched, she tried to get back the feeling from before. She thought about Ms. M's amazing jump shots, the tennis game, the sun and shade, the bird sounds Sadie would have loved. She remembered the splintery park bench, the witch's crooked smile and silly hat. The yummy peanut sauce.

Gliding back into the kitchen with her empty plate, she saw her mother alone at the table. One cup of tea, one saucer of mac and cheese, one fork.

Jess walked up behind her. Draped her body over hers. Her mother gave Jess's arms a big squeeze.

"I know it's early, honey, but I'm thinking of going to bed pretty soon."

"Okay, but don't kiss me good night. You have truffle breath!"

Chapter 13
Mothers and Daughters

Jess got into her pajamas, but not under the covers. She grabbed a comic book and tried to read, but every little sound distracted her:

A car going by (not Ms. M).

A dog barking (not Ms. M).

The toilet flushing (probably not Ms. M).

A breeze moving the branches of the walnut tree (possibly Ms. M?).

A *meow* . . .

"Onyx!"

She lifted the window screen, and in he came, leaping to the bed, turning in a circle a few times, and rolling onto his back. Jess rubbed his tummy. "Where's Ms. M?"

The cat twisted out from under her hand, thumped down to the rug, and stood near

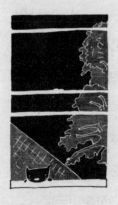

the door. "Okay," Jess said. "But we have to be quiet. Mom's probably not asleep yet."

She followed Onyx down the carpeted stairs and into the family room, where Ms. M was in the process of unfolding the blanket. "I tried to convince him to come in with me," the witch said. "But he's athletic. He wanted to climb."

"What about Mom's allergies?" Jess asked.

"Thank you for reminding me!" Ms. M reached beside the couch and lifted the cauldron lid. "I'm trying a slightly different aromatherapy recipe tonight. Less sage, more eucalyptus."

A sweet, prickly odor filled the room. It reminded Jess of a forest. As if the outdoors had come in. "That actually smells good.

Unlike the macaroni and motor oil Mom tried to feed me for dinner. I think she was kind of disappointed that I didn't go 'Yum!' and grab a spoon."

The witch sat down heavily. "Mothers and daughters. Mine wanted me to be just like her. I've never seen anyone so organized. She alphabetized everything. Baseball bats next to the beets. Peppermint right beside the porcupine."

"You had a pet porcupine?"

"Not for long. 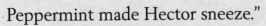 Peppermint made Hector sneeze."

Onyx jumped onto the witch's lap, wound around inside her arm, and laid his head against her heart. Jess knelt on the floor in front of them and stroked the cat's face, right under his ear. "Ms. M, do you and your mom still fight?"

"Constantly. Or not at all. Depending on how you look at it." She gently slid the sleeping Onyx onto the couch cushion. "Whenever she visits, she rearranges everything in my cupboards. Then when she leaves, I arrange it right back the way it was." Ms. M leaned forward and tugged at her pointy shoe. "Would you give me a hand, dear?"

Jess wrestled off one shoe, then the other. "Red socks. Cool."

"To harness the energy of the physical world. Ethel gave them to me last Christmas." The witch wiggled her toes appreciatively.

"I've been thinking about Ethel a lot lately. And now all this talk about cupboards has me missing my little house."

Worry fluttered in Jess's chest. "You aren't leaving, are you?"

"Goodness, no. I never travel at night."

Just then Jess's mother called from upstairs. "Jess? Are you watching TV?"

Jess hurried to the door. "I'm getting a drink."

"I thought I heard voices."

"I was telling the water to hurry up and get cold."

"Well, get your drink and come back to bed. I have a long day tomorrow. I need to be rested."

Ms. M placed her hat on the floor beside

her shoes, squeezed in next to Onyx, and pulled the blanket up to their chins.

"See you Friday, Ms. M," Jess whispered.

"Or sooner," said the witch in a sleepy voice.

"But you'll be gone in the morning, right?"

The answer was a soft snore.

Chapter 14

Schnriwisvheirecnkwilbel

Sadie and Maya came over right after breakfast. Jess led them into the family room.

"Ms. M and Onyx slept here last night?" Sadie's eyes narrowed. "I can't believe they  were here for two whole days, and you didn't tell us."

"I tried," Jess explained. "The phone wouldn't let me."

"Hmmmm." Sadie paused. Then she shrugged. "With Ms. M around, that makes perfect sense."

"Let's check and make sure the sleepover didn't leave any evidence for your mom to find." Maya got down on all fours and scrutinized the carpet. "Like a hairball."

Sadie examined the cushions.

Jess reached deep into the couch. "Look at this!" She held up what she'd found. "A dragon's tooth from Ms. M's black bag!"

"That's a tortilla

chip," Maya said. "From the Pleistocene era."

Jess dropped the fossil into the wastebasket next to the desk.

Sadie shook out the blanket. Held it to her nose. "It smells like her a little."

"What does she smell like?" Maya asked.

"It's kind of hard to describe." Sadie was quiet for a moment. "She smells nice. Like . . . dusty gingerbread, maybe?"

"Or sweaty gingerbread." Jess grinned. "Especially after a close game of HORSE."

"I hope I get to meet her soon," Maya said, perching on the edge of the desk. "Maybe Friday."

"Don't count on it," said Jess glumly. "The only reason Mom let you guys come over is to keep me out of her way while she bakes.

Friday I'm back to being grounded."

"But you ate tofu," Maya argued. "Your sentence should be reduced for good behavior."

"But it wasn't Mom's tofu. So apparently it doesn't count."

From the kitchen came the sound of pans clanging, and then a loud "Drat!"

The door to the family room flew open, and there was Jess's mother, waving her cell phone at them. "What is wrong with this thing?"

"Did you get cut off?" said Jess.

"No. I was talking to Chef Paul. One of his line cooks is out sick, and he needs me at the restaurant for an hour or so. Then I tried calling Cindy to come over and watch the cakes, but this silly thing won't work. Listen!"

The girls leaned in. *"Schnriwisvheirecn-kwilbel."*

"Gibberish," said Jess's mother. "It's on the kitchen phone, too."

"Ms. M speaks gibberish!" Jess exclaimed.

"I'm sure she does, but that doesn't help me at the moment. I need Cindy or Becca to take the last two cakes out of the oven while I'm at Chef Paul's."

"We could do that," said Jess.

Her mother actually wagged her finger. "No, no, no, no."

"Why don't you call Ms. M? Her best friend, Ethel, used to be a baker."

"Except Ethel is a bird now," blurted Sadie.

"Abroad now," Maya said quickly. "Traveling. In Europe. Or . . . someplace."

Jess's mother sagged against the nearest wall. "I don't know what to do. I don't want to disappoint Chef Paul, but this catering job is important."

"Who are all those cakes for?" Sadie asked.

"A group called AAAA. For their annual meeting. They promote animal rights. I think." Jess's mother sighed and stared forlornly at her phone. "I need to deliver the cakes to the Fairmount Hotel ballroom by two thirty, and I'm barely on schedule as it is."

"Call Ms. M," Jess urged.

"Anything's worth a try." Her mother checked her contact list. Pressed the number. "It's ringing!"

And ringing. And ringing. And ringing . . .

Wait, was that the doorbell?

Jess had a good feeling as she ran to open the front door. "Ms. M!"

"Ms. M!" Sadie shrieked, and she leaped into the witch's already open arms.

"Ms. M," Maya said, her eyes wide. "Wow."

"Oh, Ms. M, thank heavens, you're here," said Jess's mother as she joined them in the entryway. "If you could help me out this afternoon, I'd be eternally grateful. The cakes only have fifteen minutes left in the oven, but Chef Paul needs me right away."

From her pocket, Ms. M pulled a red-and-white-checked apron and tied it over her dress. "Not to worry. Ethel and I have baked dozens of sheet cakes."

"Terrific. Let me take you in the kitchen and show you what to do." The girls started to follow, but Jess's mother stopped them. "I want you to stay out of Ms. M's way. Far, far out of her way." She turned toward the witch. "Can you be firm with them?"

The witch assembled a serious expression. "I will be firm. Unyielding. Even obdurate."

"Obdurate," Maya repeated. "O-b-d-u-r-a-t-e."

Jess's mother managed a small smile. "I think firm will be enough." She and the witch disappeared into the kitchen.

"Ms. M looks different than I thought she would," Maya mused. "Taller. And it's not just the hat."

"She makes a big impression," Sadie agreed.

A few minutes later, Jess's mother appeared, buttoning her chef's coat and giving Jess a hurried kiss on her way out the door.

The car had barely turned out of the driveway when Ms. M emerged from the kitchen. She clapped her hands. "All right! Who's ready to help?"

Chapter 15
Animal Advocates

"No way." Jess shook her head vigorously. "We can't. You heard what Mom said."

"I did, indeed," said Ms. M. "She said you girls should stay out of my way." The witch spread her arms and spun in a circle, apron strings flying out behind her. "See, you're not obstructing me at all!"

"You know what she meant."

"No great chef works alone." Ms. M wobbled a little as she came to a stop. "Chef Paul must have at least a half dozen assistants in his kitchen right now. Including your mother."

"She has a point," said Maya.

"It would be really fun," said Sadie.

"Yeah, but—"

Ms. M stood in front of Jess. She covered Jess's smooth hands with her own slightly gnarled ones. She looked Jess straight in the eyes.

Hey, Ms. M's eyes are hazel, Jess thought. *Just like mine*.

"Pretty please," said the witch. "I could use the help."

Jess took a deep, steadying breath. "Maybe."

The kitchen was warm and smelled amazing. Metal baking racks spread across the counter beside the stove.

When the timer dinged, Ms. M reached into the pocket of her apron. Out came two spotless white oven mitts. "They're woven with genuine ice from Iceland," she said as she pulled them on. "That's what the catalogue says."

"Won't they melt?" asked Maya.

"I reorder frequently. Now stand back, everyone!" She opened the oven door. A wave of cocoa- and vanilla-scented air rolled into the room. One at a time, she set the last two cakes on racks beside the others.

She leaned across the row of cakes, five in all, and inhaled. "The merest hint of citrus and, unless I miss my guess, a touch of sour cream. Your mother has a real gift, Jess."

Jess shrugged. "It's just cake. She makes cake all the time."

"Nonetheless." Taking off her oven mitts, Ms. M pointed to the rather lopsided chocolate cake on the center rack. "We can't use that one. Let's test it to make sure the rest are sweet enough. And no forks! You don't know where those forks have been. Fingers only."

They all tasted, licked their lips, tasted again. "Scrumptious," declared Maya.

Just then the phone rang. As Jess reached

for it with a chocolate-smeared hand, Ms. M said, "Tell your mother not to worry."

"Hi, Mom. Ms. M says not to worry. Everything's fine." Jess listened. Held out the phone to Ms. M. "She wants to talk to you."

The witch listened. Nodded. Listened some more and finally said, "Leave it to me." She put down the phone and adjusted her hat, making sure it stood straight up. "So. Someone else failed to show up for work and Chef Paul is overwhelmed. Your mother needs us to do the frosting."

"Us?" Jess raised her eyebrows.

"She suggested chocolate frosting on the white cakes and white frosting on the chocolate cakes, but that sounds so conventional, don't you agree?"

"What do you mean?" said Sadie.

"She means boring," Maya translated. "Should we do something different?"

Jess began to pace. "Wait a minute. What if we screw up? I'll be grounded forever. Maybe longer."

"I remember the time I helped Ethel make chocolate mousse for a fancy dinner party," said the witch in a faraway voice. "Only we accidentally made chocolate mouse instead. People are still talking about it."

"I bet." Jess laughed. Then she said, "It *would* be cool to make an animal cake, since this group likes animals."

"This chocolate frosting is pretty dark," said Maya, staring into one of the big

dessert!?

CHOCOLATE MOUSE

stainless steel bowls. "We could make a panda. Or a zebra."

"Eurasian magpies are black and white," offered Sadie. "And they're smart. The only bird species that can recognize itself in a mirror."

"So we'd put all the cakes side by side and carve out wings—" Maya began, but Jess interrupted.

"That will look like a kindergarten art project."

All four of them were silent. Waiting for inspiration.

Ms. M said, "Ethel and I once made an Alp for a witch from Switzerland. Chocolate cake on the bottom and vanilla on top. We even made mountain climbers out of mini-marshmallows."

"That gives me an idea," said Jess. "I've still got my old Safari Game. It has all kinds of little plastic animals."

Sadie clapped her hands. "We could make a habitat! And find places for the animals. Caves and ledges and stuff. Like a diorama. I bet animal advocates would love that!"

"Nobody move," said Jess. She dashed toward the stairs.

In her room, Jess found the box right where she'd remembered it—top shelf of her closet, under Chutes and Ladders and her collector's album of baseball cards. Dad had helped her put away the game last time they'd played. Now, standing on tiptoe, she could reach it all by herself. She slid the box from the pile, headed for the door, and . . .

Stopped.

She could almost hear her mother. *Read the recipe. Measure carefully. Sift twice.*

Maybe they should do what Mom wanted, after all. Maybe she and Sadie and Maya should go outside and play basketball and stay out of Ms. M's way.

On tiptoe again, about to put the game back, she remembered something Dad always said: *Every trip to the batter's box is a fresh start.*

So they'd struck out with the lasagna. So what?

Safari animals stared up at her from the cover of the box. Jess addressed them directly. "All right, guys. Ready to hit a home run?"

The giraffe seemed to stand up taller.

The lion roared.

The gorilla pounded his chest.

The elephant raised her trunk in an enthusiastic salute.

Down the stairs Jess went, through the living room, and toward the kitchen, where her friends were waiting to decorate the best cake ever!

Chapter 16

Time to Move a Mountain

After the cakes cooled, the girls washed their hands and went to work. Sadie divided the white icing with a spatula. Maya added green food coloring to half. "That should be enough for vegetation. We'll use the white at the top for snow."

Jess surveyed the line of animals on the

counter. "I don't have anything that lives in the snow."

"We'll put the mountain gorilla up there," Maya said. "He'll be visiting his yeti friend."

With a look of intense concentration, the witch placed the last layer of cake on the stack. She braced the mountain with one hand and plopped chocolate frosting onto it with the other.

Sadie grabbed a butter knife and started spreading. "This already looks so much

better than some boring checkerboard."

"It seems kind of unsteady," Jess said, frowning.

"The icing will hold it together," Ms. M said. "You'll see."

Jess pressed her thumb against the impala's horn, watched the tiny dent it made slowly disappear. "I sure hope so," she murmured.

"You need to stop worrying," said Maya. "And hand me a mammal."

Fifteen minutes later, they all stepped back. An elephant and a giraffe roamed the foothills. A small herd of zebra grazed. A hippo lay on its side in a chocolate mud bath.

"How about a cave for the leopard?" Sadie suggested.

Maya picked up a big spoon and carved

out a hole. "Except, turn him around," she said. "Nobody wants to eat dessert looking at a leopard's butt."

Jess wandered over to the pantry. "If we had some blue food coloring, we could make a river for the crocodile to swim in and drag unsuspecting swimmers into the depths."

While they hunted for the food coloring, the kitchen phone rang. Ms. M picked it up, listened for a bit, and said, "Not a problem. Of course I can drive a van. I have a commercial driver's license." She hung up and said brightly, "Change of plans! Your mother still can't get away from the restaurant, so we're going to meet her at the fundraiser. Time to move a mountain, girls."

Carefully—very carefully—Maya and

Sadie carried the cake to the J. B. Catering van while Jess stacked cookbooks on the driver's seat. Ms. M climbed in and settled on top of *The Joy of Cooking*.

"Can you see?" asked Jess. "Do your feet reach the pedals?"

The witch squirmed a bit, gripped the wheel, and leaned forward. "Almost. One more cookbook should do the trick. How about *Lo-Cal Treats*? It's thin."

Once Ms. M was situated, Jess joined her friends in the backseat of the van. "How's the cake?"

Sadie answered, "The giraffe fell over, but he's not hurt."

Maya added, "The lion was going to eat him, but we got there just in time."

Up front Ms. M wiggled and sat up tall. "Perfect." Then she slipped to one side.

Jess leaned over the seat. "Maybe we should call a cab."

"Don't be silly. Just center me, dear. And turn the key, please—I can't quite reach it. Wonderful. Off we go!"

Ms. M checked the rearview mirror before backing slowly down the driveway. She turned right on Belmont, left on Oxley.

The honking started immediately.

"You might want to speed up a little," said Jess, staring out the back window in dismay at the growing line of cars.

"I get the Mature Driver's Discount from my insurance company. I'm not putting that in jeopardy just because someone's pants are on fire."

Jess looked at her watch. "But we only have ten minutes!"

That's when they heard the siren. A police car, lights flashing, cruised up behind the van.

Jess buried her face in her hands. *Strike one.*

The witch glided to the curb and turned off the engine. A police officer in sunglasses appeared at the window. "Do you know why I pulled you over?" he asked.

"I was being a bit too careful, wasn't I?" said the witch.

"You were going six miles an hour."

"I will go faster, I promise."

"Your driver's license, please."

When the witch opened her black bag to get her wallet, a bat flew out and escaped through the open window. The officer waved his arms around and slapped at his helmet. "What the heck was that?"

"What was what, officer?" asked the witch

innocently. She handed him a laminated card.

He studied it. Studied her. Studied the card again. "This is a Transylvania driver's license. How in the world did you get that?"

"Look again, young man."

"Oh, yeah. Pennsylvania. I could have sworn . . . in any case, I'm going to have to write you up. Driving too slow is as much of a hazard as speeding."

"There's not one chance in a hundred that you will give me that ticket," said the witch.

The officer chuckled. "I didn't say go a hundred. But twenty-five miles per hour would be nice."

He began to write. Stopped. Shook his pen. "Doggone it. I'm out of ink. Don't go anywhere."

The witch started the van.

Jess's heart flip-flopped into her socks. "Didn't you hear what he said?"

"Aren't you the one who's in a hurry?"

Strike two.

All four of them turned around to watch as the policeman tugged at the driver's side door of his black-and-white Ford. Next he tried the door on the passenger's side. He tried the rear door. He tried all the doors again. None of them budged.

The officer stomped back to the van. "Something's haywire with my cruiser. Just get on out of here. But consider yourself warned."

"Thank you," said the witch, shifting into DRIVE and oozing back into traffic.

She handed Jess her driver's license to put away.

"Did you make his pen not write and lock his car doors?" Jess asked.

"How could I do that? I was sitting right here with you. Now put that license in my wallet before I lose it."

"It does say Transylvania!" Jess exclaimed. She showed it to Maya and Sadie.

"Of course it does," said the witch. "My Pennsylvania license expired ages ago."

Chapter 17
Dessert!

With minutes to spare, Ms. M circled the hotel parking lot, searching for a space close to the service entrance.

Sadie pointed. "Look! Someone's pulling out."

Ms. M waited, then deftly maneuvered the van between the white lines. She turned off the engine and sat back with a satisfied sigh.

"Okay, let's go," said Jess, unbuckling her seat belt.

"Wait a moment." Ms. M rolled down the driver's side window halfway. She cocked her head to the side, as if listening. "Can you sense it? The troposphere is positively alive with information this afternoon."

"Please, Ms. M," Jess urged. "We have to be inside, like, now."

All of a sudden a bright yellow bird

perched on top of the half-open window. Ms. M exhaled loudly. "Aha!"

"Is that—" Sadie began.

"Yes," said the witch. "An evening grosbeak."

"I knew it!" said Sadie. "Don't you love the stripes on his wings?"

"He's a gorgeous specimen," the witch agreed. "Like a piece of the sun."

The grosbeak emitted a series of high-pitched chirps.

"Really?" said Ms. M. "Oh, that's wonderful. I can't thank you enough. Wait!" She reached into her black bag and came up with a handful of seeds. "Sunflower. Your favorite."

They all watched as the bird delicately dipped his head and ate one, then two, then three seeds before darting away.

Ms. M turned toward the girls and beamed. "It's very likely that Ethel has returned."

"The bird told you that?" said Maya.

"Not in those words, exactly. But the message was crystal clear."

"That's great." Jess clasped the witch's always-warm hand. "Really great. But can we focus on the cake now?"

Ms. M returned Jess's squeeze. "Certainly. I won't leave until everything's in place."

"You're leaving?" Jess wailed at the same time Sadie said, "No!" Maya threw a protective arm around them.

"I'm sorry I wasn't more specific. My sources say Ethel is home. Possibly in need. Of course it may not be true, but I have to find out." She pressed the button to raise the window. "We'll talk about this later. Right now let's get our magnificent creation inside."

With Ms. M leading the way, Jess, Sadie, and Maya pushed the clattering four-wheeled cart holding the cake toward the hotel.

"Slow down," Maya warned. "The mountain gorilla is looking a little nervous."

Sadie smoothed over a crack at the top of the leopard's cave, then another one near the impala, and licked her finger. "I don't blame him."

As they crossed the parking lot, Jess said, "There's Mom's Honda. I hope she hasn't been waiting long."

"We're right on time," said Ms. M, holding open the big metal door.

They pushed the cart down a dimly lit

hallway and into a large, high-ceilinged room with a red-carpeted floor. Peculiar paintings decorated the walls. Paintings of, well, paint, maybe? Red swirls and green dabs and yellow drips and blue gobs.

Dozens of people milled about in front of the artwork. They passed a bearded man who pushed his glasses up onto his forehead and leaned in to peer at a painting of a giant praying mantis. Or was it a skinny dancer with too many elbows?

Jess spied her mother across the room talking to a woman in a pink beret and a blue-and-green-patterned dress. "Dessert!" sang the woman as they approached with the cart. But when they came to a stop, her expression changed from delight to confusion. She tugged at her chunky yellow necklace. "What in the world do we have here?"

Jess's mother's face was as white as her chef's coat.

"It's—oh, no!" Jess let out a squeak of alarm. Because the cake was beginning to slide!

The gorilla was the first to go.

Then the avalanche began in earnest. The frigid zone crumbled into the temperate zone, which melded into a swirling mass that swept through the tropical zone. All of it toppled over the edges of the cart, rolling and roiling toward the carpet, coming to a stop at the toes of the woman's purple snakeskin boots.

Nobody moved. Nobody, it seemed, even

breathed. The room was utterly silent. Jess's mother squeezed her shoulders. Hard.

Strike three. She was out.

Jess didn't turn around to face her mother. Couldn't turn around. Didn't want to. Ever. If only she could stay frozen in that moment, staring at the leopard's butt, his head buried in a fragment of cake. Forever.

The silence was broken by a tremendous cheer and wild applause.

"Well done," someone shouted.

"Performance art at its best!" crowed the woman, shaking Jess's mother's hand. "Bravo!"

Chapter 18
Ready. Set. Go.

Back at home after dropping off Sadie and Maya, Jess and her mother collapsed onto kitchen chairs.

"Abstract artists. Not animal advocates." Her mother shook her head for the billionth time that afternoon. "I don't know how I got that mixed up."

"It was useless Vicki's fault." Jess couldn't help grinning. "She took the message."

"I know, but I should have checked. I did check. At least I thought I did. I meant to."

"You must have heard wrong."

"Apparently." Then she laughed. Again. Which started Jess laughing. Again. Which started her mother snorting and laughing even harder.

Once Jess could breathe, she said, "When

the cake went kablooey, I was scared you were going to faint. Or murder me. Or both."

"I thought it was a disaster," her mother admitted. "But they thought it was art." She shook her head for the billionth-and-first time.

"Ms. M said you'd be happy with the way things turned out."

"She's such an odd little person. Where is she, anyway? I thought she was right behind us."

"Sorry!" The witch barged into the kitchen through the back door. "I was so distracted by all the Ethel news coming in from the celestial spaces that I left this in the van." She plunked her dusty black bag on the table where it . . . twitched?

"Please don't tell me"—Jess glanced

nervously at her mother—"that you have Onyx in there."

"Would you believe me if I said I was taking a baby dragon to a friend?"

"No."

Ms. M looked almost smug. "Good. You shouldn't. It's a preposterous thing to say."

"It will certainly be less exciting around here without you, Ms. M," Jess's mother said, and then she added, with yet another laugh, "I hope." She swiveled to pull her wallet out

of her purse, which hung from the back of her chair. "Let me pay you for the last few days."

The witch waved away the offer. "Next time."

Jess perked up. So she'd be back! Maybe even with Ethel!

"Are you sure?" said Jess's mother.

The witch gave an emphatic nod as she beamed at Jess. "Friends are the real prosperity. Besides, I hate to carry cash when there's a chance it might catch fire."

"Well, all right then." As Jess's mother turned away to replace her wallet, the witch's bag expanded and opened a crack. A wisp of smoke spiraled up and out.

"Behave," hissed Ms. M. "Or no cricket snacks for you!"

"Cricket snacks?" Jess whispered.

"It's all they eat at this age." She hefted her bag onto her shoulder. "Time for us to be going."

"Us?" Jess's mother looked puzzled as she shook the witch's small hand. "Jess, you can walk Ms. M out, but come right back, okay?"

"Sure, Mom."

On the front stoop, Jess grabbed the witch's arm. "Hold on! I almost forgot. I want to give you something."

She sprinted around the side of the house to the herb garden, plucked what she needed, and sprinted back. "Here." She handed the witch the feathery strands of dill. "Ethel's favorite. For good luck. So you'll find her for sure."

Ms. M pressed the dill to her nose and took

a noisy sniff. "Ahhhh." She gave Jess a warm, snaggle-toothed smile. "I feel more hopeful already. Thank you, dear."

"Race you to the end of the driveway?"

"One moment." The witch stuffed the dill into her pocket. Clamped her hat down tightly on her head. Performed a few creaky knee bends. "Okay." She crouched in a starting position. "You're on."

"Ready. Set. Go!"

Jess flew. She skidded to a stop just past the mailbox, whipped around, and shouted, "Left you in my dust!"

The driveway was empty.

In the yard to her right, Mr. Percy pruned his lilac bush. To her left, a delivery truck idled by the curb.

No sign anywhere of a small woman in black with a bag that squirmed on its own.

"Wow! Wait till I tell Sadie and Maya," Jess murmured.

When she returned to the kitchen, her mother said, "At the risk of repeating myself, there goes an odd little person." She sipped her tea and continued, "But I'm glad you two had a good time together. And speaking of good times, Vicki will be here tomorrow,"— she held up her hand when Jess started to protest—"but you can invite Maya and Sadie over. *If* you promise to stay fifty feet away from the oven at all times. Make that a hundred and fifty feet."

"Hey, we hit it out of the park today! Out of the park, over the fence, and gone."

"True, but today was . . . " Her mother searched for a word.

"Different?" Jess suggested.

"That's one way of putting it." She leaned back, rested her head against the wall, and closed her eyes. "I should start dinner, but I don't think I can move from this chair."

Jess went over and opened the refrigerator. "We have tofu. And peanut butter. We could . . . "

Her mother grimaced. "Too much cutting and grating."

"How about this?" Jess held up a colorful refrigerator magnet. It said BAMBINI'S PIZZA. WE DELIVER.

"Mushroom and spinach?"

"Onion and green pepper."

Her mother pulled out her phone and dialed. "Yes, hello. I'd like to order a large pizza. Half mushroom and spinach, half onion and green pepper. Fifteen minutes? Perfect."

After she hung up, she wrapped her arm around Jess's waist. "I should have told them to make absolutely sure my spinach does not touch your onion."

Jess leaned toward her mother. Breathed in the faint scents of vanilla and cocoa powder and shampoo. "That's okay. They're all vegetables. They'll get along."

Ms. M's Tips for Young Chefs

Cooking, like petting a baby dragon, can be dangerous. Never do either without first getting permission from a parent or other adult guardian.

Start with clean hands and a clean cauldron.

Tie back your hair or wear a tall, pointy black hat.

If you have a toad in your pocket, return him to the terrarium.

Read the recipe **all the way through** before you begin, to avoid frustrating surprises, such as realizing you should have soaked the magic garbanzos for Jack's Beanstalk Casserole overnight.

Regarding flavorings and spices, be bold. Say the recipe calls for cobweb jam, but you prefer grape. Why not make the switch? Unlike spells, recipes usually give you room to experiment. Ethel could explain, but she's . . . well, you know.

Becoming a good chef takes practice. What you make may not look or taste like the perfect photo in the cookbook. Wait, did you taste the photo? Don't do that.

If Onyx wanders by, call me! If your own cat or dog wants to play a bit, take a break.

Tidy up the kitchen when you're finished. Your lazy broom may refuse to help. Tell him he can't have dessert.

Ms. M's Spellbinding Grilled Tofu with Thai Peanut Sauce

A local witch is the best helper, but if she's away, then a parent or another adult will do. Here's what you'll need:

¼ teaspoon finely chopped or grated ginger root

2 large cloves of garlic, finely chopped

¼ cup cilantro (plus a few extra sprigs for garnish—that's cooking talk for decoration)

3 tablespoons peanut butter

1 tablespoon lime juice

½ teaspoon red or green curry paste (or more, depending on how much spice you like)

½ tablespoon soy sauce (probably more—but not too much!—if you're using unsalted peanut butter)

1 cup coconut milk

16 ounces extra-firm vacuum-packed tofu, drained and patted dry, cut into ½-inch slices

1. Start by combining the ginger root, garlic, and cilantro with a mortar and pestle, if you have them. If not, you can just toss these three ingredients right into a saucepan over low heat, and stir once or twice. Don't they smell bewitching together?

2. Next add the peanut butter, lime juice, curry paste, and soy sauce, and stir to combine. At this point, the mixture will be spoon-stands-up-in-it thick. Trickle in some coconut milk. Stir. Trickle in some more. Stir again. Is it starting to look like a sauce? Keep going!

3. Now place the tofu slices side by side in a nonstick skillet. Have your helper grill them on the stove for about 3–4 minutes on each side, until they are just starting to turn golden brown. Crispy edges are really good. While that's happening, the sauce can be heating slowly in the pan.

4. The tofu goes on a colorful plate. The sauce goes on the tofu. The extra sprigs of cilantro go on the sauce. Once cooled a little, it all goes in your mouth. (Well, not the plate.) The sauce also tastes marvelous on raw or cooked veggies—bell pepper slices, broccoli, mushrooms—and noodles. Onyx likes it best on salmon and, who knows, you might, too.

Get to Know
Your Herbs

Cilantro: Looks a little like parsley, but a sniff will sort that out! Cilantro is very zesty. It's the only herb with a nickname: coriander. Used frequently in Mexican food, especially *Estofada de Bruja* (Witch's Stew).

Dill: Has fine leaves with flowers shaped like umbrellas. And dill is more than just pickles. Try it on potatoes! Yum. The name means "to calm or soothe." Upset? Have a pickle and chill.

Mint: It's everywhere! Toothpaste, gum, breath mints. Ethel liked to freeze sprigs of mint in ice cubes, making lemonade twice as tasty. Mint is bossy, though, and the plants can take over a garden.

Rosemary: Smells very forest-y and looks like a sprig from an evergreen tree. Good for memory. Study for a spelling test with rosemary nearby. Take a bit to school. During the test the scent will remind you how to spell *abracadabra*.

Sage: Its fuzzy, long, narrow leaves have a peppery smell that might remind you of turkey and dressing, but try a little in an omelet. Just a little. Sage is potent! Do you have a secret wish? Write it on a sage leaf and put it under your pillow. Especially powerful if you are wishing for Thanksgiving.

Thyme: Makes friends easily and is often seen bundled up with bay leaves and parsley. Thyme is a bravery herb. Put some in your socks if you have to walk past a bully. Plus, its lemony-woodsy scent will give you sweet-smelling feet.

Magic Books

Cook, Deanna F., illustrated by Michael P. Kline. *The Kids' Multicultural Cookbook*. Charlotte, VT.: Williamson Books, 2008.

Dahl, Roald, Felicity Dahl, and Josie Fison, illustrated by Quentin Blake. *Roald Dahl's Revolting Recipes*. New York: Puffin Books, 1997.

Gold, Rozanne, illustrated by Sara Pinto. *Kids Cook 1-2-3: Recipes for Young Chefs Using Only 3 Ingredients*. New York: Bloomsbury, 2006.

Katzen, Mollie. *Honest Pretzels: And 64 Other Amazing Recipes for Cooks Ages 8 & Up*. Berkeley, CA: Tricycle Press, 2009.

Tierra, Lesley, illustrated by Susie Wilson. *A Kid's Herb Book*. San Francisco: Robert D. Reed Publishers, 2000.

Waters, Alice, with Bob Carrau and Patricia Curtan, illustrated by Ann Arnold. *Fanny at Chez Panisse: A Child's Restaurant Adventures with 46 Recipes*. New York: HarperCollins, 1992.

Yolen, Jane, and Heidi E. Y. Stemple, illustrated by Philippe Beha. *Fairy Tale Feasts: A Literary Cookbook for Young Readers and Eaters*. Northhampton, MA: Interlink Books, 2009.

Magic Links

Hey, Kids, Let's Cook! (A Children's Television Production):
www.heykidsletscook.com

Spatulatta: www.spatulatta.com